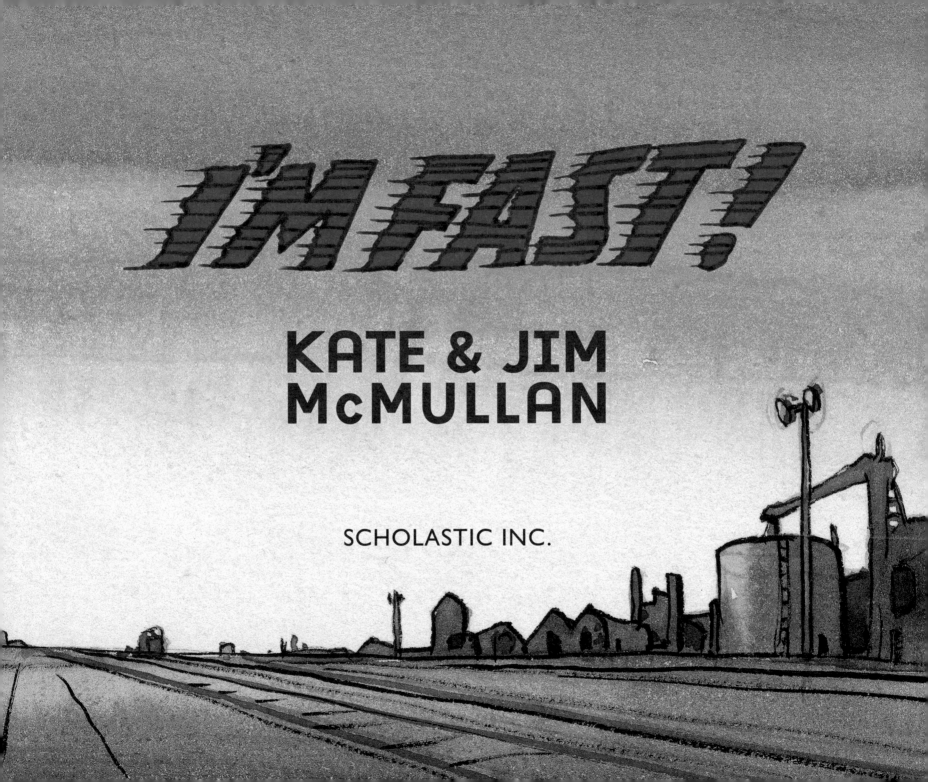

I'M FAST!

KATE & JIM McMULLAN

SCHOLASTIC INC.

ISBN 978-0-545-58019-9

Text copyright © 2012 by Kate McMullan. Illustrations copyright © 2012 by
Jim McMullan. All rights reserved. Published by Scholastic Inc., 557 Broadway,
New York, NY 10012, by arrangement with HarperCollins Children's Books, a division
of HarperCollins Publishers. SCHOLASTIC and associated logos are trademarks
and/or registered trademarks of Scholastic Inc.

12 11 10 9 8 7 6 5 4 3 2 1   13 14 15 16 17 18/0

Printed in the U.S.A.   40

First Scholastic printing, March 2013

For Anika & Carter Petruccelli

Thanks to the HarperCollins crew, Alessandra Balzer, Ruiko Tokunaga, Sara Sargent, Jenny Rozbruch, Carla Weise, and Kathryn Silsand, for keeping us ON TRACK, and a big TOOO-OOOO to Holly McGhee, Joan Slattery, and Elena Mechlin over at Pippin.

SACRAMENTO

Vrrrrrrrrrrrrrrrrrrum!

What's that, Red?
You wanna have a RACE?
Vrrrrrrrrrrr-rum!
First one to Chicago wins?
You're on!
Lemme load my FREIGHT.

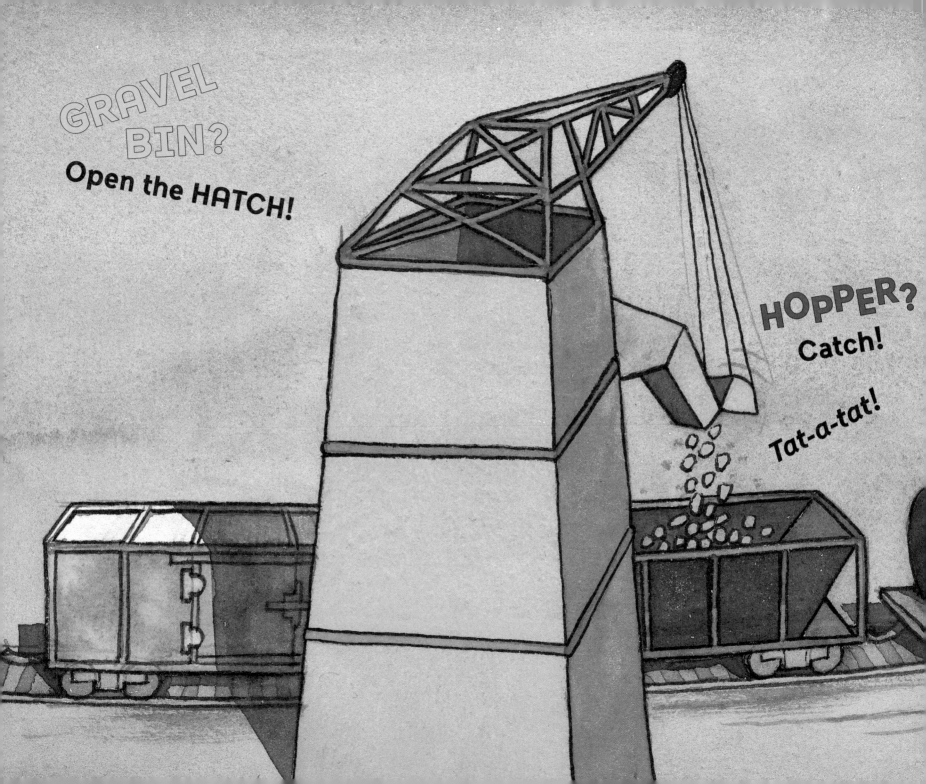

FULL SPEED AHEAD
through the tunnel—

TOOOOOOOOOO!

Chooka chooka chooka chooka

Outta the DARK,
into the—

SNOW!

So? **PLOW** right through it.

Car? Can't do it—
Nothin' to it for a

FREIGHT TRAIN!

Choo-ka Choo-ka Choo-ka Choo-ka

Chooka chooka chooka chooka

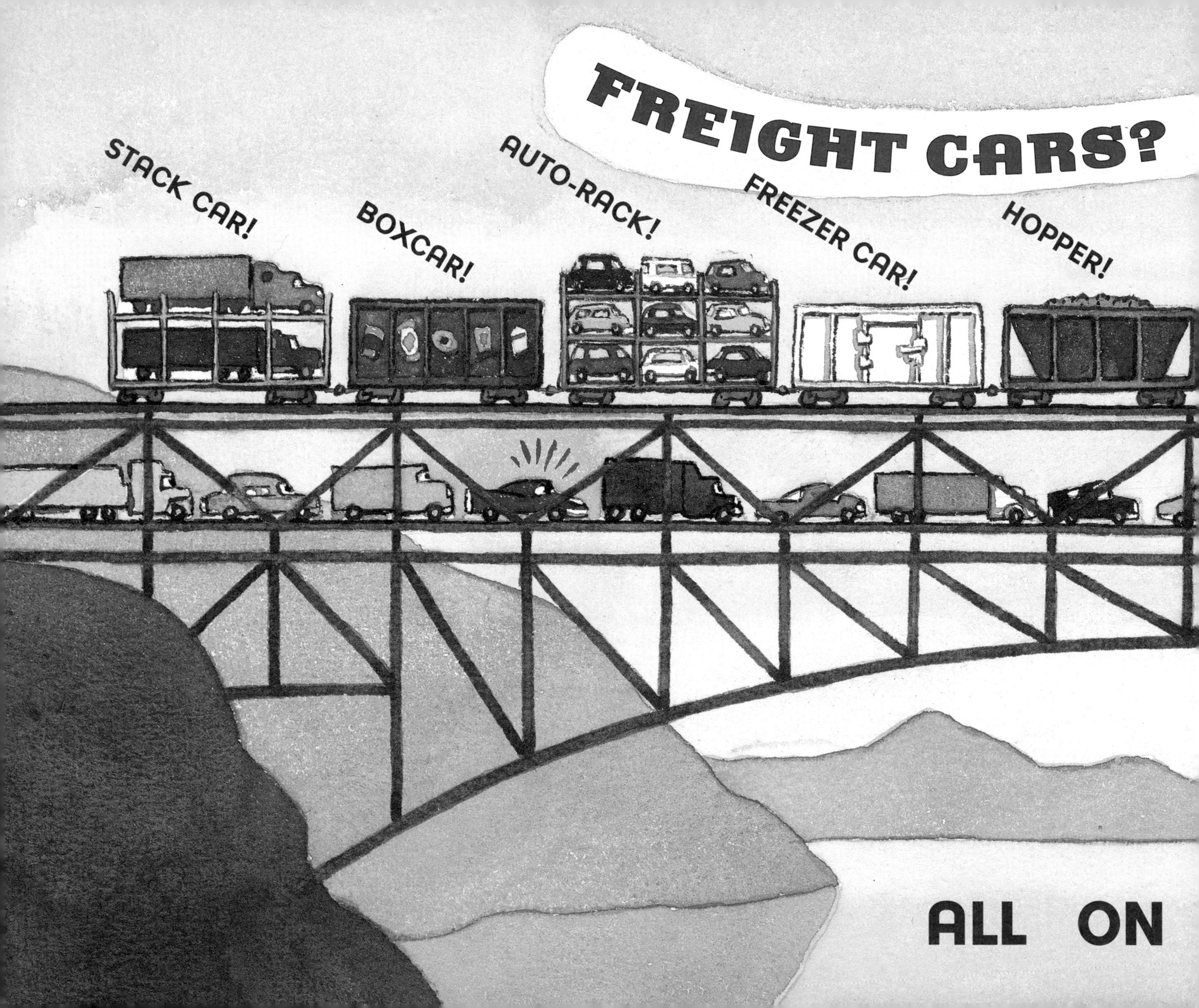
FREIGHT CARS?
STACK CAR!
BOXCAR!
AUTO-RACK!
FREEZER CAR!
HOPPER!
ALL ON

Onto the SIDE TRACK, **THROTTLE BACK.**

Won the race to Chicago—

YESSSSSSSSSSSSSSSSSSSSSSSSSSSSS!

Take the **TRAIN**, Red!
Yeah, roll on up!
I'll get you there—

FAST!